Go to www.maxflash.co.uk
and enter this code:
JH3OPS11LB29
for your freebies, downloads
and other Max Flash goodies

For Janice and Steph

STRIPES PUBLISHING
An imprint of Magi Publications
1 The Coda Centre, 189 Munster Road, London SW6 6AW

A paperback original
First published in Great Britain in 2009

Text copyright © Jonny Zucker, 2009
Illustrations copyright © Ned Woodman, 2009

The right of Jonny Zucker and Ned Woodman to be identified as the
author and illustrator of this work respectively has been asserted by
them in accordance with the Copyright, Designs and Patents Act, 1988.

ISBN: 978-1-84715-082-0

All rights reserved.

This book is sold subject to the condition that it shall not, by way of
trade or otherwise, be lent, resold, hired out, or otherwise circulated
without the publisher's prior consent in any form of binding or cover
other than that in which it is published and without a similar condition,
including this condition, being imposed upon the subsequent purchaser.

A CIP catalogue record for this book is available from the British Library.

Printed and bound in Belgium.

2 4 6 8 10 9 7 5 3 1

MAX FLASH
MISSION 5
CHAPTER 1

The wave was gigantic – at least ten metres high, and it was hurtling furiously towards him. Max was well out to sea, the California shoreline just a wavy scribble of sand in the distance. He could hear the hiss and roar of the water crescendo as it smashed onwards.

Max took a deep breath as the wave sped nearer. What he did in the next few seconds was absolutely crucial. It didn't matter that he was an excellent swimmer and could hold his breath longer than most people on earth – if he timed things wrong, the crashing water would pulverize the life out of him and hurl him down, deep under the ocean's surface.

With strong strokes, Max paddled forward and as the swell of water picked him up he leaped to his feet. He rode down the face of the wave, building up speed. Then the foaming crest curled over him.

From the shore Max couldn't be seen at all. But as the wave broke on the surface of the ocean, he flew out of the roaring tunnel of water, unhurt and utterly ecstatic.

"AWESOME!" he yelled, punching the air with delight.

Surfboarding champions of the world watch out!

Max could just make out his parents on the beach in the distance, sunning themselves on loungers. He was about to swivel round on his board and go hunting for the next thunderous wave when he heard a metallic beep from his sunglasses. He pressed a tiny black button on the underside of the frames. Immediately a mini plasma screen slid down over the right lens.

The face of a woman with tightly scraped-back blonde hair and ice-cool blue eyes appeared on the screen. It was Zavonne, and she looked deadly serious.

CHAPTER 2

Zavonne worked for the DFEA (Department for Extraordinary Activity). The DFEA dealt with all matters that couldn't be trusted to the official authorities. If shadows came to life or aliens from the planet Krystal 76 reached the earth's atmosphere, the DFEA would get in there first and 'clean up' before the authorities even realized something weird was happening.

Max's parents were stage magicians and had carried out two missions for the DFEA, but Max had now completed *four*. Zavonne had recruited Max because of his incredible abilities as a contortionist and escapologist. He was also a fine performer of illusions, a talent he'd picked up from watching, and then participating in, his parents' stage shows. His DFEA missions so far had involved travelling inside a computer hard drive, visiting a distant galaxy, defeating evil sea creatures and taking on mummies brought back from the dead.

On seeing Zavonne's face, Max felt a mixture of disappointment and excitement. *Come on, Zavonne, I'm only on day three of my Californian Christmas holiday!* But then he began to wonder – *What kind of mission might she have in mind for me this time?*

"Over the last couple of years," said Zavonne, without so much as a hello, "a number of explorers have gone missing in a remote region of the Antarctic known as the Bolt Zone – named after Sir Travis Bolt, the explorer who discovered it."

Missing explorers in the Antarctic – cool, or should I say freezing!

"The international authorities charged with overseeing this particularly inhospitable part of the world believe that the missing explorers died of hypothermia. Their bodies, however, have never been found."

"Buried under snow?" asked Max.

"That's one of the theories. The wind-driven snow blizzards out there can be vicious. However, over the years there have been several rumoured sightings of strange snow beasts in the region."

Snow beasts?

"What, like the Abominable Snow Man?" said Max, grinning.

Zavonne ignored his comment. "The DFEA appreciate these are only rumours, but have always had an interest in the area."

Water lapped at Max's surfboard and he paddled with his right arm to steer the board away from an incoming wave.

"There are currently three scientists at the Bolt Zone Research Station. Dr Savalle Klosh and Dr Marion Holroyd are both very experienced and are at the station for a five-year project monitoring climate change. Dr Stella Jenkins is only there for a few months, on her own research project. Ten days ago, the three of them noticed that the temperature in the area had dropped to an *unusually* cold level for this time of year. It's summer at present in the Antarctic and the days are very long, with up to twenty hours of daylight. An average temperature for this season is about −8°C, but it had dropped to −30°C, a temperature more usual for the winter months. The scientists predicted it would rise back to its normal parameters within twenty-four hours, but this did *not* happen. Instead the temperature has continued to fall. By last night it was registering −50°C."

"What do the scientists think is causing the drop in temperature?"

"They, along with the Antarctic authorities, believe that extreme winds are responsible for this drop and predict that matters *will* right themselves shortly. But even as we speak the temperature is continuing to fall. If the temperature carries on falling and reaches −100°C, there will be an eco disaster on an unprecedented scale. Ice will spread thousands of miles beyond its usual boundaries, affecting water supplies and crops. In short, this will have a huge knock-on effect for the rest of the world."

Max looked around at the clear water, amber sun and turquoise sky. The Antarctic was a seriously long way away from his current sun-drenched location.

"In fact," Zavonne went on, "the temperature drop has already had consequences."

"In what way?" asked Max.

"Two nights ago," replied Zavonne, "a British navy vessel on a training exercise in the region, travelling less than three miles away from the Bolt Zone Research Station, sent out a distress signal. I'd like you to take a look at it."

Zavonne's face disappeared from the screen and was replaced by a fuzzy picture of a bearded man wearing a navy blue jacket garlanded with medals. He looked extremely anxious.

"This is Captain Edward Hartnell of *The Triumphant*," he said gravely. "I am issuing a MAY DAY signal. In the last ten minutes, the ship has been surrounded by thick sheets of ice that formed at a terrifying speed. We are unable to navigate in any direction, and are facing the threat of—"

Suddenly the screen went blank.

Zavonne's face reappeared. "There was no more contact with Captain Hartnell after that," she said. "The navy got a rescue helicopter out there as quickly as it could, but they found no sign of any crew members. The navy have now dispatched an icebreaker to the scene to prise *The Triumphant* loose and tug it back to dock, where it will be examined. They believe the ship's crew must have set out for the research station and perished on the way."

"But you don't agree?" asked Max.

Zavonne shook her head slowly. "We believe

that the extra-freezing conditions and the
disappearance of the crew are linked in some
sinister way," she replied. "And that, Max, is
where you come in."

MISSION 5

CHAPTER 3

Zavonne is sending me to the Antarctic!

"I want you to go out there immediately and
a) find out why the temperature is falling, b)
ensure that it doesn't reach −100°C and c) find
out what happened to *The Triumphant*'s crew."

So, no pressure then!

"You will be based at the research station,
and your first job will be to get on board *The
Triumphant* and look for clues as to the crew's
whereabouts before the icebreaker turns up."

"Er, small point," said Max, "how am I going

to get into the station? I don't exactly look like a fully qualified climate change expert, do I?"

Zavonne pursed her lips. "Your cover story is that you are working on a student project about global warming. You will be reporting your findings back to an international student committee. Doctors Klosh and Holroyd would not be keen on having a child shadowing them, but Dr Jenkins has been contacted and is fine about your visit. It goes without saying that she knows absolutely nothing about the DFEA or our activities, and it's vital that things stay that way."

"Is it just Jenkins, Klosh and Holroyd at the research station?" asked Max.

"No," replied Zavonne. "A television survival expert called Gruff Addison is also stationed there with his cameraman, Jim Sweeney. They're filming his next series."

Gruff Addison! The *Gruff Addison! Only the coolest man in the history of TV, who can live*

for weeks in freezing snow caves, wade through ice lakes and treat his own frostbite? The man is a legend!

Max was thrilled at the thought of meeting his hero and wanted to question Zavonne further. But then he remembered something.

"What about my gadgets?"

"Return to your hotel room and await further instructions," Zavonne ordered.

Her face then disappeared from the screen.

MAX FLASH
MISSION 5
CHAPTER 4

Twenty minutes later, Max was back in his hotel room with his parents. There was a knock on the door. Max hurried across the room and opened it. A man in motorbike gear stood on the threshold.

"Package for Max Flash?" he enquired, holding out a sparkling silver briefcase.

Max nodded and signed for the delivery. Once the door was closed, he opened the briefcase. In one half was a small all-terrain backpack, top-of-the-range snowsuit, extra-thick gloves, UV-filtering sunglasses and a pair of high-spec snow goggles. Max's mum and dad watched as he pulled out each item and inspected it.

"Cool!" he beamed.

In the other half of the briefcase were three padded envelopes: one blue, one green and one red.

"Open the blue one," instructed Zavonne's voice.

Max spun round. Zavonne's face was suddenly on the screen of his TV.

Is there anywhere she can't get to?

He opened the blue envelope and pulled out a pair of tiny in-ear black headphones.

"Those are ICE-CUTTER HEADPHONES,"

explained Zavonne. "If you find yourself needing to cut through ice, place the two ear pads against the surface about thirty centimetres apart. If you press on the earphones, they will cut out a circle of ice one metre in diameter. They work with ice up to a thickness of fifty centimetres."

Nice one, Zavonne!

"Now open the green one," she instructed.

Max fished inside the envelope and pulled out what looked like a standard pack of mint chewing gum.

"That is a GUM-SHOOTER STUN GUN," said Zavonne. "When you rip off the top, three more packets will snap out to form a 'gun', with a trigger on the underside. This 'gun' fires Crash Bullets. The bullets will stun opponents for ten seconds, buying you time for your next move. You can use the gun for a maximum of twelve rounds, after which it will become inoperable."

ICE-CUTTER HEADPHONES

0.60

0.20

1M

50M

GUM-SHOOTER STUN GUN

MINTO

02   20

02

10

12 X 1 CRASH
BULLETS

10

0   08

BACK-FIRE BOOSTER

50
30

*A gum gun!
Excellent!*

Max didn't wait to be asked before tearing open the red envelope. Inside was what looked like an extra-compact sleeping bag.

"That is a BACK-FIRE BOOSTER," stated Zavonne. "The booster can be attached to your backpack like a normal sleeping bag, but it contains a powerful motor and fuel. Pull the white toggle and you will then be fired a hundred metres through the air at a maximum height of twenty metres."

Flying? Yes!

"But remember," said Zavonne.

"I know, I know," retorted Max. "The gadgets can only be used when I'm in extreme danger or facing death."

"In the backpack there's a map showing the positions of the research station and *The Triumphant.*"

"So, when am I off?" asked Max.

"There's a small airport fifteen miles from your hotel," said Zavonne. "A plane is waiting for you there. This will take you to Chile, where you will switch to a helicopter and be transported to the Bolt Zone."

Max's dad went over to the dressing table and grabbed the key to the hire car.

"The Antarctic is a dangerous and hostile territory at the best of times," warned Zavonne. "There's a strong possibility you will be facing terrifying and unknown forces. And you will be working against the clock. I repeat that the temperature must NOT be allowed to reach −100°C."

Bring it on, thought Max, as he examined his gadgets. When he looked up, the TV screen was blank and Zavonne had vanished.

MAX FLASH

MISSION 5

CHAPTER 5

"Be extra careful, Max," said his mum anxiously, as they walked over the tarmac at the tiny airport to the four-seater plane. Max was wearing his backpack and carrying a holdall containing his snowsuit and cold weather gear.

"Look after yourself," said Dad. "It'll be really, really cold out there."

"I thought it was going to be baking hot," quipped Max.

Dad gave him a look.

"OK," promised Max, "I'll be extra careful."

His parents hugged him goodbye, and Max hurried towards the plane. The DFEA pilot, a tall guy with a square jaw, took Max's holdall and slung it into a storage unit. Ten minutes later, as the plane soared into the air, Max saw his parents waving from the ground. He took a deep breath.

Will I be coming back alive or will I freeze to death out there?

The flight to Chile went quickly. They touched down at another airport, where a helicopter was waiting. Even though it was hot, Max changed into his snow gear; he'd need it soon.

The helicopter was incredibly noisy and Max had to wear ear protectors, which meant he couldn't talk to the pilot or listen to music on his mp3 player. So he gazed out of the window and watched as they flew first over the desert, then the ocean and finally over huge ice sheets.

"That's the Bolt Zone Research Station," shouted the pilot, pointing down to three large red rectangular structures. They were interconnected by a series of transparent tunnels and stood on a platform raised above the ground by giant steel pylons. Beneath the pylons at ground level was a large grey cube, connected to one of the red structures by a long ladder. On the roof of one of the buildings was a large dome. On top of the others were three wind turbines and rows of solar panels.

"I can't land, so you'll have to use the ladder," the pilot shouted, flicking a switch. A small panel on the side of the helicopter slid open, letting in a gust of ferociously cold air. The pilot pressed a button and a metal ladder shot out through the opening, dangling down towards the snow-covered ground. Max threw his holdall from the helicopter and checked his backpack was strapped on tightly.

"I'll take you as low as I can go," said the pilot. "Good luck."

Thirty seconds later, Max lowered himself over the edge of the helicopter and started climbing down the ladder.

Everywhere around him was blindingly white: the ground, the mountains in the distance – everything. As he reached the bottom rung, he saw a figure emerge from one of the red buildings, head down a walkway and hurry over towards him. Max jumped down and his feet smacked on to the frozen ground. The ladder immediately shot back up into the helicopter and it sped off.

"Dr Stella Jenkins," said the figure, smiling and reaching out a ski-gloved hand to shake Max's. "Let's get you inside."

The scientist was much younger than Max had expected. She had large brown eyes, a small button nose and strands of blonde hair pushed out from beneath her black snow-hat.

Max picked up his holdall from the ground and then followed Jenkins up the walkway. She tapped a code into a steel panel on the wall and a door slid open. As they crossed the threshold, it slid shut behind them.

The first thing Max noticed was the cold. He'd expected it to be far warmer inside the station, but it didn't feel much different from outside.

"Isn't it a bit chilly in here?" he asked.

Jenkins nodded. "I'm sure you're aware of the rapidly lowering temperature situation," she replied. "Well, the station's heating system is also on the blink. Great timing, right! We keep fixing it, but it keeps on breaking down again – we can't work it out."

Max studied his surroundings. He was in a large laboratory – the first red building. To his right was a workbench lined with microscopes and test tubes. Gleaming silver machines with black dials covered the wall on the far side of the room. To his left was a row of grey industrial thermometers with different calibrations, each giving a reading of –55°C.

The temperature is still falling – bad news!

In the middle of the lab was a long wooden

table on which were three computers, along with various notepads, journals and digital printouts.

"There's no internet connection out here," said Jenkins, "but we do have satellite communications equipment." She pointed to a couple of large black machines that looked like ultra-sleek DVD players, with a slim, high-tech microphone attached.

At least we're not totally cut off from the rest of the human race!

Across the room, Max spotted a huge mesh of unconnected, different-coloured wires. Jenkins followed his gaze. "Some equipment was stolen recently," she said.

"Out here?!" exclaimed Max.

"Yes, a few of our industrial thermometers. Weird, huh?" said Jenkins. "There's a research station further down the coast, but it's well over a hundred miles from here. Anyway, what would they want our equipment for?"

Jenkins took Max through a door on the far side of the lab into a transparent tunnel, which led to the second structure. The first room had two sofas, three comfy chairs, a bookshelf crammed with scientific volumes and a TV.

"The living room is where we relax," explained Jenkins. "Mind you," she added, lowering her voice, "Klosh and Holroyd aren't exactly what you'd call the relaxing type."

Max laughed – Jenkins was all right. He followed her into a small kitchenette, with a long, narrow table flanked by stools.

"The dining room," she announced. "The food here is just about bearable," she grinned, "but you need to be a fast eater!"

Before Max could ask what she meant by that, they'd moved on again, through another see-through passage. They were now in a corridor with three doors on either side.

"The bedrooms," said Jenkins. "Small but comfortable."

She pushed open the furthest door on the right. "This one's yours."

There was just about enough space for a bed and a narrow wardrobe, while in the corner there was a small temporary heater. "Dump your stuff and come and meet the docs," said Jenkins. "They're on the roof. We'll pop up for a quick hello."

Max dropped his holdall on the floor, then followed Jenkins up a metal ladder at the end of the corridor. They climbed through a trapdoor at the top and stepped out on to the flat roof Max had seen from the helicopter. Crouching down beside a long line of tiny individual solar panels was a portly man with a round face and a long moustache, and a thin woman with pale blue eyes and a short grey bob. They were deep in conversation.

"Dr Klosh, Dr Holroyd," said Jenkins. "This is Max, the young man I was telling you about. He's come out here to shadow me for that international student project."

The scientists looked up, and Max gave them his most winning smile.

"Hello, Max," said Dr Holroyd.

"Hello, Max," said Dr Klosh.

"Doctors Klosh and Holroyd designed these new solar panels," explained Jenkins. "They not only provide a good power source, especially in the summer when we have twenty hours of daylight, they're also excellent at melting ice very quickly. Which, as you can imagine, is extremely useful out here."

The scientists had already returned to their work.

Thanks for the big welcome!

"Don't worry about them," whispered Jenkins. "That's just their way – they're always like this."

Max would have liked to ask Klosh and Holroyd about their thoughts concerning the radical temperature drop – after all, they were the experts. But he sensed that now might not be the right moment. Jenkins was already heading back inside. Making sure the

scientists were still caught up in their discussion, Max quickly bent down, picked up one of the solar panels and dropped it into his backpack.

You never know when this might come in handy!

"Is Gruff Addison around?" he asked Jenkins hopefully, when they reached the bottom of the metal ladder.

"Our great TV celeb," smiled Jenkins. "He's out on a shoot with Jim. Are you a fan of his?"

"Kind of," said Max, trying to hide his disappointment.

They headed back to the laboratory. "Right, I've got to get back to work," said Jenkins. "I've got some interesting rock sediments to examine. You're welcome to watch."

"Er, if it's OK with you I'd like to get started on my project right away – you know, explore the local area," replied Max.

Starting with The Triumphant *to see if I can find any clues to the crew's disappearance.*

"Sure," nodded Jenkins. She reached over, grabbed a couple of small plastic containers and handed them to Max.

"Collect a couple of snow samples while you're out there," she said. "We can look at them later."

Max tucked the containers into one of his snowsuit pockets. Jenkins slid open a large panel in one of the lab walls. It opened out on to a ladder that led to the grey cube. They climbed down and Max found himself in a large storage room crammed with equipment. He spotted four gleaming silver snowmobiles, several pairs of skis, extreme weather clothing, snowboards, ice picks – pretty much everything you'd need to explore a freezing wilderness.

Jenkins walked over to a rack. "What would you prefer," she asked, "skis or a snowboard?"

Max didn't think twice. "A snowboard," he replied.

He'd never been on a snowboard before, but he was pretty sure he'd be able to transfer his surfing skills. Jenkins handed him a sleek blue snowboard, a pair of extra-tough brown snowboots and a pair of lightweight snowshoes to fit over the top. "The snowboard snaps in two so you can store it in your backpack when you're climbing," explained Jenkins.

Ten minutes later, Max had positioned his snowboard on a ledge of snow next to the station. He checked his snowsuit pockets and felt his gadgets nuzzling safely inside.

"Don't stray too far!" called Jenkins, climbing back up the ladder to the station.

"I won't!" cried Max.

He checked the map Zavonne had given him to make sure he knew how to reach *The Triumphant*. Then he pulled down his goggles and launched himself down the slope.

CHAPTER 6

Woohoo!

Max had been skiing a couple of times, but
snowboarding was way more exciting. It was
a bumpier journey than on skis, but it was
totally exhilarating and he picked up speed
quickly. He turned left and right, getting used
to the feel of controlling the board.

This is wicked!

He sped past towering mountains threaded
with hundreds of narrow crevices and
enormous sheets of glistening ice.

*This is like another planet – and I should
know because I've been on other planets!*

He raced through a deep valley and a few
minutes later reached the base of a huge
mountain. He snapped the snowboard in two
and tucked it under his arm; he'd be needing
it again soon.

Trekking to the summit of the mountain
took about half an hour. When he got there
he stood looking out over the edge at the
vast expanse of ice below that stretched as
far as the eye could see. About a hundred

metres from the shore, and trapped in its freezing grip, was *The Triumphant*.

Max fastened his feet on to his snowboard again and flew down the other side of the mountain. He stopped when he reached the shoreline, got off his snowboard and placed it in his backpack, which he stashed next to a snow-covered bolder. After putting on his snowshoes, he stepped carefully out on to the frozen ocean and slowly approached the huge ship. The nearer he got, the more he was amazed by the sheer size of the vessel.

There were small portholes at least twenty metres above him, and they all looked tightly shut.

How inconsiderate to close all of the possible entry points!

He walked slowly around the edge of *The Triumphant* until he finally spotted a porthole that was a tiny bit ajar. Max took off his snowshoes, then grabbed at a jutting-out metal bolt and pulled himself up, planting his snowboots against the side of the ship. Their superb grip held firm. He stretched out for another handhold and pulled himself higher. A couple of minutes later, he was positioned right next to the porthole.

He pulled at the window to see if he could prise it open a little more, but it didn't budge. He tried this a few more times, and on his fourth go he managed to create a small gap. Taking a deep breath, Max began to squash his arms and shoulders into his body as tightly as

he could. When his upper body was
compressed to half its usual
width, he pressed his head
against the porthole and
started, very slowly, to
squeeze it through the
gap. It was a close thing
and Max could feel the
metal rim digging into his
skull, but when his head
finally slipped through, the rest
of his body followed quite smoothly.

*Now let's get on with finding some clues as
to the crew's whereabouts.*

As Max straightened up he took in the room
he'd entered. It contained four bunks – sailors'
quarters. The cabin was incredibly neat, with
one large trunk stored under each bed. He
stepped out into a corridor and entered the
cabin next door. It was exactly the same as
the first.

He returned to the corridor and headed for a large door at the far end. Stepping through, he climbed a flight of steps, which took him up and out on deck. It was a vast expanse, with wheels and pulleys and rigging spread over its surface and lifeboats clinging to its sides. Max looked around.

Still no sign of any life.

He hurried along the deck and reached some glass double doors. He pulled them open and found himself on the ship's bridge. There was a central control console covered in hundreds of buttons and dials, a computer work station, then gaps where a couple more must have been – with wires sticking out. Max stared at the loose wires. He thought back to the missing equipment at the research station. Was it the same thief who'd stolen from both the station and *The Triumphant*? And, if so, how did they get in? And what were they up to?

He left the bridge and carried on walking, right over to the other side of the deck. Climbing down a twisting flight of steps, he reached a corridor and halted abruptly.

In front of him was what remained of a door. It had been smashed into thousands of fragments, which now lay scattered all over the floor. Max stepped through the splintered hole into the room. It was four times the size of the other cabins.

These must be Captain Hartnell's quarters, or at least they were...

The place was a complete tip. Tables were overturned, chairs were smashed to bits, papers were strewn all over the floor. A cabinet had been pushed against the door as a barricade, but this too lay in pieces.

Talk about utter devastation!

There were hundreds of oily marks all over the floor, mainly boot prints. But then Max noticed that some of these were much larger than the others. He placed his foot beside one; it was three times bigger than his own. Not only that, the large prints were footprints – and each foot seemed to have seven toes!

Was that what happened? Were the crew attacked by some kind of giant seven-toed beasts? Had they barricaded themselves in here to try and fend off their attackers?

Max shivered.

Could any of the creatures still be on board?

He pulled out his digital camera and took several shots of the giant footprints. There didn't appear to be any further clues as to the identity of these attackers, so he hurried back to the sailors' quarters, squeezed through the open porthole and eased himself down to the ground.

But the second his snowboots touched the ice, there was a great cracking sound as a circular sheet of ice flew up into the air, leaving a large hole about ten metres away. Max gaped at the hole in astonishment, his heart racing. He was about to put on his snowshoes when a second circle of ice shot upwards, creating another large hole, much nearer this time.

Without hesitation, he started to run.

CHAPTER 7

SMASH! Another hole was punched through the ice, less than five metres away. CRASH! CRASH! Two more were smashed out, revealing the icy ocean below. Without snowshoes the surface was even more treacherous and slippery, and he had to work extra hard to stop himself from toppling over.

Max fled towards the place he'd left his backpack. *At least I know that's where I'll find solid ground.* As he ran, multiple holes exploded all around him.

He jumped, skidded and swerved to avoid them; it was like running through sniper fire. He had seventy metres to cover before he made it back to shore. But then Max's right foot suddenly slipped and he fell, sliding straight towards one of the holes.

Noooooooooo!

He dug his left snowboot into the ice and managed to stop a couple of centimetres shy of the hole. Struggling back to his feet, he ran on. There was ice spraying all around him now, crashing against his body and his head. With thirty metres to go, a huge line of holes burst open just in front of him.

My route's being blocked!

His whole body was tense with determination as he ran onwards, picking up speed. Then he launched himself into the most powerful long jump he could manage. As his body arced through the air over the huge gap, he looked down into the icy water below.

If I fall in there I'm finished. I have to make it!

To his incredible relief, his feet smacked down on to solid ground. He turned back to look at the ocean. The sheet of ice between him and *The Triumphant* was pockmarked with holes.

He stood there panting, thoughts racing around his brain. *Someone or something wasn't too pleased about my investigations on board* The Triumphant. *Was it the creatures that attacked the crew? And who or what made all those holes in the ice?*

MAX FLASH

Max put on his backpack. For a moment all was silent and still, but this didn't last long. Suddenly, there was an ominous creaking sound. Max turned to see *The Triumphant* breaking free from its icy shackles.

The holes have broken the ice's grip on the ship!

With a terrible groan, *The Triumphant* began to plunge downwards. Thirty seconds later, it disappeared below the water line.

I guess the navy's icebreaker won't be much use now.

Max stared out at the space where the ship had been. He thought back to the seven-toed footprints he'd seen in the captain's quarters. Maybe there'd be some more footprints in the snow, which might lead him to whatever it was that had attacked *The Triumphant*. He started following the shoreline to his right.

As he went he studied the ground. Unfortunately, the only thing he could see was snow. He stopped when he'd gone five hundred metres and returned to his starting point. He went left this time, but still no prints.

Max shook his head. With the temperature still dropping he needed leads and fast. What had Zavonne said? *The temperature must NOT be allowed to reach −100°C.* He began to tramp up the mountainside overlooking the coast – again, not such an easy task without snowshoes. When at last he reached the summit, he looked down at the valley he'd passed through earlier and pulled the snowboard out of his backpack.

Max placed the board on the ground and stepped on to it, adjusting his foot bindings until he was comfortable. But then he spotted something in the snow. He crouched down to take a closer look.

Yes! A seven-toed footprint. And it looks pretty fresh.

Max glanced round, but there was no sign of any life. He scooped up some snow from the footprint and emptied it into one of the plastic containers Jenkins had given him. He put the container into one of his snowsuit pockets and gazed into the valley.

There was another print and another. Max launched himself down the slope. He'd followed the trail about a hundred metres when he suddenly heard a faint rumbling sound from somewhere high to his left. He glanced up and in the distance he could just make out the shapes of two large white figures. They were far too big to be humans. But his gaze quickly shifted to the sheet of snow that was hurtling down the valley in his direction.

No way! An avalanche!

MAX FLASH

MISSION 5

CHAPTER 8

Max was already too far down to climb back up to the peak he'd just come from. And he'd never be able to reach the other side of the valley. He was trapped, with a great mass of snow sweeping down towards him.

How bad would that be – to escape from certain death in the frozen ocean only to be buried by an avalanche!

He shifted his weight to swerve to the right and leaned forward to up his speed.

I'm never going to make it!

Max began to feel the panic set in, but he suddenly remembered his gadgets. He reached behind him and pulled on the toggle of his BACK-FIRE BOOSTER.

This better work!

The frontline of the avalanche was seconds away – descending at phenomenal speed. But the instant he pulled the toggle there was a loud popping noise and he was suddenly fired up into the air. A split second later, the avalanche flooded into the valley, engulfing everything in its path. Shooting forward at incredible speed, Max yelled with delight and relief as he flew above it.

After a hundred metres he dropped down on to a mountain ridge. The snowboard hit the ground and Max let it run for a few seconds, then swerved to a stop.

He watched in silence as the last of the snow crashed down into the valley. The entire path through the middle section of the valley was now completely buried.

Talk about a lucky escape!

Max studied the mountain ridges for the huge figures he'd seen earlier, but there was no sign of them. He had a strong feeling that these creatures were the same ones who'd attacked *The Triumphant*, and he was pretty sure that they'd had a hand, or paw, in starting the avalanche.

He had a final look around, and then turned and headed back to the research station, eager to check out the snow samples he had collected. On returning, Max left his backpack, snowboots and snowboard in the grey storage cube, then headed for the lab. He checked the thermometers: –59°C. Max frowned.

How on earth am I going to stop the temperature plummeting so fast when I don't know what's causing the drop?

There was no one around, so he pulled the plastic container out of his pocket and emptied the snow sample on to a glass slide. He slipped this under a microscope on the workbench and placed his eye to the viewing glass. He spotted it immediately – a long, coarse white hair, far too long and thick for any human.

It must belong to one of the seven-toed creatures.

"What have you got there?"

Max was startled by Jenkins's voice. He looked up as she walked across the lab.

"Er, it's just a bit of snow," he replied.

"So you managed to get some samples?" she asked. "Here, let me take a look."

"It's OK," Max replied, a little too quickly. "But thanks."

"No problem," she said, with a slightly puzzled look.

Max scooped the snow sample back into the container and slipped it into his pocket.

"I've got some data that compares the Bolt Zone with other regions of the Antarctic," said Jenkins. "I think you might find it useful."

Max groaned inwardly. He didn't have any time to look at data, but he couldn't keep turning down Jenkins's offers or she'd get suspicious. So he spent the next half-hour pretending to look at spreadsheets, while keeping an eye on the thermometers, which had dropped to −61°C.

"Thanks for that," said Max finally. "Is there any chance I could check out the snowmobiles – I've never been on one before."

He'd decided that while snowboards were brilliant fun a snowmobile would be far quicker, especially for going uphill.

"Sure," nodded Jenkins, reaching over to a hook on the wall and pulling off a key. "This key'll work for all of them."

Max hurried down to the storeroom. He flicked a switch on the wall and a floor-to-ceiling steel shutter opened. Then he settled himself on to one of the snowmobiles and turned the key. The engine screamed into life. He twisted the handlebar throttle and the machine leaped forward through the exit and on to the snow.

Superb!

He turned the handlebars and the snowmobile went to the left. He yanked the handlebars hard and skidded to his right. Max then increased his speed and spun the vehicle through a 180° turn.

This is awesome!

He turned round again and was about to put the machine through another spin when a furious voice cut through the chilled air.

"WHAT ON EARTH DO YOU THINK YOU'RE DOING?!"

It was Dr Klosh.

He was standing in the storeroom entrance, eyeing Max angrily.

"THOSE VEHICLES ARE FOR RESEARCH TRIPS ONLY – NOT FOR PERFORMING MOVIE STUNTS!"

Max gulped and killed the engine.

"Sorry... I was just..."

"I'm sure he'll be using it for research," cut in a deep voice. "And anyway, I thought the 180° turn was worth watching!"

Max recognized the voice instantly. He spun round and there was Gruff Addison, all six foot four of him, with his trademark chunky frame, goatee beard and piercing blue eyes. Beside him was an equally large guy with a full beard and a v-shaped dimple on his chin.

Saved by the earth's number one survival expert!

Dr Klosh frowned at Gruff's intervention. "All right," he muttered, "but no more fancy stuff, thank you." He turned and started climbing back up the ladder to the lab.

Max dismounted.

"Hi," said the TV star with a wide grin, "I'm Gruff Addison."

I know who you are!

"And this is my cameraman, Jim Sweeney."

"Howdy," said Jim, with a nod of his head.

"You're the kid who's come out here to shadow Jenkins, right?" asked Gruff.

"Yeah, I'm Max. Thanks for stepping in."

"No worries," smiled Gruff. "Klosh can be a bit earnest."

Max laughed.

"Right," said Gruff, "Jim and I are going inside to check out the rushes we filmed this afternoon; fancy taking a look?"

"Definitely," nodded Max, trying not to sound *too* enthusiastic.

MAX FLASH

MISSION 5

CHAPTER 10

Max, Gruff and Jim sat in the living room watching some incredible footage on a small playback monitor attached to Jim's camera. Here was Gruff Addison leaping off a sheer mountain face on to a sheet of ice; there he was disappearing into a great mound of snow; there he was again, skidding across the bottom of a dangerously sloping crevice.

This is unbelievable, and I get to see the unedited TV footage with the great dude himself!

Max had a million questions to ask Gruff and was disappointed when Jenkins poked her head round the door to say that dinner was ready.

A short while later, Max was sitting at the dining table with Doctors Jenkins, Klosh and Holroyd, plus Gruff and Jim. Klosh had obviously calmed down after his earlier outburst, so there was no further mention of Max's antics on the snowmobile. Jenkins had prepared the supper – vegetable lasagne.

At first Max was taken aback by the speed at which everyone tucked into their food, but looking down at his plate he saw the reason why. His portion had come out of the oven piping hot, but was already starting to freeze at the edges.

So that's what Jenkins meant when she said you had to be a quick eater here!

He'd taken a look at the thermometers before supper and they were touching –65°C.

It seemed to Max like it was almost that cold inside the station as well.

There was quiet for a while as everyone chewed. Max saw an opportunity to dig for info. "You know this temperature-dropping situation," he began, directing his comments at the scientists. "Are you still pursuing the theory that it's connected to freak wind chill?"

"It's the *only* possibility," replied Holroyd, "but we're shocked by the *speed* at which it's dropping."

"I'm not sure wind chill is the only explanation," said Jenkins thoughtfully. "I think there may be something else going on; it's kind of scary."

Max swallowed. *Has she discovered something weird out here, too?*

"Come on, guys, let's not panic," cut in Gruff. "A temperature of –65°C isn't the end of the world. I was stranded at –85°C on an ice shelf once, for 48 hours. Sure, I nearly died and it was weeks before any sensation returned to my fingers and toes, but I'm still here, aren't I?"

Max looked at the TV explorer with admiration. *This guy is awesome!*

After supper, Max helped Jenkins clear the table. When they'd finished, she spent some time playing with the heating system, which was situated in a cupboard in the corridor outside the bedrooms. Max watched as she used a screwdriver to twist a series of dials and prise some levers upwards.

"I've fixed it," she announced after about ten minutes. "It should at least last through the night."

"Nice one," nodded Max.

"I'm going to crash out," said Jenkins.

"Really?" asked Max. He glanced out of the window. It was still light, but when he looked at his watch it said 10.10p.m.

Jenkins laughed. "You'll get used to it."

She went into her room and Max headed off to bed, too.

I better get some sleep and be fresh for the morning. I HAVE to get some leads tomorrow!

It was too cold to get undressed so he put on his thermal pyjamas over his clothes, then dived into his microfibre sleeping bag. The day's exploits had left him totally exhausted and it wasn't long before sleep reeled him in.

Max woke with a start. He checked his watch –
3.20a.m. blinked the digits. Out in the corridor
he could hear a faint tapping sound. He turned
over and tried to go back to sleep, but the
tapping kept him awake. So he climbed out of
his sleeping bag and stepped out into the
corridor to investigate. Standing in front of the
heating system cupboard, with his back to
Max, was Gruff.

"Everything OK?" asked Max.

Gruff jolted with surprise and spun round.

"Oh, hi, Max," he said, "you startled me."

"Sorry," said Max. "What are you doing?"

"It's the heating. I know Jenkins fixed it earlier, but it's gone again."

"But she said it should at least last through the night," said Max.

"Did she?" said Gruff. "Well, it's obviously in a worse state than she thinks! I guess the tapping woke you, yeah?"

Max nodded.

"Well, I haven't been able to fix it this time. You get used to hardships when you're out here."

"I can imagine," said Max.

"There was this time I had to bury myself in an ice tunnel to avoid a mad snowstorm," laughed Gruff. "I must have been in there for at least twelve hours – thought I might freeze to death; kept my mind busy by thinking about the husky races I've competed in!"

The guy is more than a legend!

"I was impressed by the way you handled the snowmobile earlier," said Gruff. "And not everyone can cope with these conditions, but it seems like you're doing pretty well. You could have a future in the TV survival industry!"

Me! Become like Gruff! Supreme!

"Anyway," said Gruff. "I'm off back to bed."

"Cool," said Max, nodding goodbye and returning to his room. He climbed back into his sleeping bag and slept well for the next few hours, dreaming about being a top survival expert with his own TV show.

When he got up he found Jenkins in the kitchen preparing breakfast. "I can't believe the heating broke in the night," she complained.

"I know," agreed Max. "Gruff tried to fix it, but had no luck. How about asking Klosh or Holroyd?"

"They're already out on a field trip," said Jenkins.

Just then Jim passed through the kitchen.

"Want some breakfast?" asked Max.

"Can't hang around," said Jim. "Gruff and I are off to film at a gorge. Gruff's going to do some freefall ice leaps!" Jim pulled a small vial out of his pocket, with some sort of green liquid inside. He lifted it to his mouth and pulled a face as he drank it down.

"What's that?" asked Max. "Some kind of extreme weather energy drink?"

"Yep, something like that," replied Jim, as he went through the door. "See you guys later."

Max prepared himself a bowl of cornflakes and snaffled them down before the milk froze.

"Come and check out some snow level footage recorded by the cameras in the Viewing Dome," said Jenkins, when he'd finished eating. Max sighed inwardly.

I desperately need to get out there and continue my investigations.

"Er, OK," he replied hesitantly.

The Viewing Dome was accessed via a ladder.

It contained lots of different-sized telescopes, but Jenkins insisted they watch some pre-recorded footage of snow levels in the vicinity. This was on the tedious side of ultra boring. Finally, Jenkins went to make some hot drinks and Max found himself alone.

He stepped over to the largest telescope and stared through the glass. Outside, a wind had picked up and was beginning to blow snow around. But then, through the snow, Max caught sight of two shapes. There, not more than a hundred metres away from the station, were two huge beasts. They were at least seven feet tall and their bodies were covered with thick coats of white fur. Their eyes were huge and crimson, and sunk back into deep eye sockets. Their teeth were as sharp as daggers. And they had seven toes.

Max sprinted down the ladder and hot-footed it towards the lab. But as he went through the tunnel outside the kitchen he ran into Jenkins, almost knocking the two piping hot mugs out of her hands.

"Where are you going?" she asked in confusion.

"Nowhere," Max called back. "I just need to ... get a bit of fresh air."

Max grabbed the snowmobile key from the lab. Then he dashed down to the storeroom, picked up his rucksack and opened the steel shutters. He leaped on to the nearest vehicle and started up the engine.

At the sound of the snowmobile, the two snow beasts turned and started to run.

They're frightened!

The creatures had a hundred-metre start and they were running fast, but they'd be no match for a snowmobile.

The wind was howling and snow swirled around him. Max hadn't got far when suddenly he heard a revving sound behind him. He glanced back. It was Jenkins! Her curiosity had obviously got the better of her. She was catching up fast on one of the other snowmobiles.

Disaster! She'll see the beasts, freak out and my cover will be blown!

It was an agonizing dilemma; should he turn

back to stop her seeing the snow beasts, or should he keep chasing them? It was too valuable a lead, so he sped on, hoping to lose Jenkins in the snow storm.

Up ahead the beasts disappeared over a high ridge. A few seconds later Max's snowmobile flew over the ridge and came smashing down on the other side with such force that he was thrown off. The vehicle skidded to a halt a short distance away, and a dazed Max got to his feet. He was standing on a wide, icy plateau and there, not more than ten metres away, stood a group of *six* snow beasts, including the two who had led him there. But they didn't seem frightened any more. They looked menacing and dangerous. One of the beasts raised his fists in the air and let out a deep, ear-splitting roar.

How could I have been so stupid? The snow beasts wanted me to follow them! It's an ambush!

MAX FLASH MISSION 5

CHAPTER 12

A second later, Jenkins came flying over the ridge. She too was thrown off her snowmobile, which crashed into Max's vehicle and came to a stop. She struggled to her feet.

"Run!" yelled Max, but it was too late. Jenkins had caught sight of the six snow beasts.

"W-w-what are they?" she asked in a quivering voice.

But Max had no time to explain because at that second the beasts pounced. Jenkins screamed and stood frozen to the spot. Max acted instantly. He pulled out his GUM-SHOOTER STUN GUN and ripped off the top. At once the packet of gum transformed itself into a sleek weapon. He squeezed the trigger hard and six bullets flew out, sending the snow beasts flying backwards.

Max headed for the snowmobiles, pulling Jenkins with him. But the beasts were back on their feet and beginning to advance again. He fired off another few rounds, sweeping the gun through the air and scattering bullets amongst the beasts. They were stunned and disorientated, and this gave Max and Jenkins a valuable few seconds to reach their vehicles.

Max turned his ignition key and hit the throttle. The snowmobile roared into life and shot forward. When he'd gone ten metres he quickly glanced round to make sure Jenkins was following him. But she wasn't.

For some reason her machine hadn't powered up. And all six beasts were tearing towards her. Max spun through 180° and pulled the trigger on the SHOOTER; nothing. He'd used all twelve rounds!

There was only one thing for it. He pushed down on the throttle and clung on like crazy as his snowmobile flew forward. Jenkins saw what he was doing and leaped out of the way. The beasts didn't react as quickly and Max's machine ploughed straight through them, sending them flying in different directions.

"GET ON!" yelled Max, reaching out a hand.

Jenkins grabbed his hand and jumped on to the snowmobile. Max gritted his teeth as the vehicle shot forward.

"THEY'RE COMING AFTER US!" shouted Jenkins.

He looked back and saw that the beasts were gaining on them. This would have been bad enough, but Max heard a sharp snapping sound and spied a crack opening in the ice up ahead. The ground was splitting in two! If they didn't move fast, Max and Jenkins would be stranded on the wrong side of the crevasse – at the mercy of the snow beasts!

And the gap was widening by the second.

"FASTER!" screamed Jenkins, looking back in terror.

Max twisted the throttle as hard as he could, accelerating towards the widening gap. He could hear the thundering of the beasts' paws pounding behind him. The snowmobile was now going so fast that its front lifted off the ground. As it crashed through the air with the deep crevasse below, Max closed his eyes.

Please make it! Please make it!

As the snowmobile began its downward trajectory, he opened his right eye and, to his immense relief, saw that they were about to land on the other side.

"WE DID IT!" he yelled triumphantly, turning back to look at Jenkins as the vehicle smashed on to the ground.

But to his horror, the seat behind him was empty.

CHAPTER 13

A mighty blizzard was now raging and Max could only just make out Jenkins on the other side of the crevasse. She was being dragged away by the snow beasts.

"NOOOOOOOOOOO!" Max screamed, slamming on the brakes. The snowmobile twisted violently and he had to use every morsel of his strength to turn it round to face the crevasse. He hit the throttle, intent on flying back over the gap towards Jenkins and her captors. But the vehicle made a wheezing sound and refused to pick up enough speed to propel him over. It must have taken a bad hit on landing, which had affected its power. Max hit the handlebars in frustration and fury.

Zavonne's going to kill me. I've blown my cover and I've got a scientist kidnapped by snow beasts!

Max drove along the edge of the crevasse as quickly as his snowmobile would allow, but there was no passing place between the two sides of the chasm and no further sign of Jenkins.

After searching for two hours, it was an exhausted and very cold Max Flash who finally headed back to the station. The first things he saw when he walked into the lab were the thermometers. They were registering –84°C.

The temperature's heading towards –100°C fast, and as well as trying to stop it getting there I now have to rescue Jenkins, not to mention finding out what happened to the crew of The Triumphant.

He went to the living room, frantically trying to weigh up the pros and the cons of contacting the emergency services on the satellite communications equipment. On the one side, he badly needed help. But how seriously would they take him when he reported that Jenkins had been kidnapped by seven-toed snow beasts? He entered the lab deep in thought, but just as he reached the satellite communications equipment Gruff walked in.

"You look terrible," said Gruff. "What happened?"

Max stopped and leaned against one of the work surfaces.

Maybe Gruff can help me. He knows this terrain better than anyone.

"It's Dr Jenkins," said Max quietly, "she's gone."

"Gone?" asked Gruff. "What do you mean gone?"

Max paused for a second.

Will Gruff believe me?

Max sighed deeply. "We were attacked," he replied. "By these ... snow beasts. They dragged her away."

"Snow beasts?" Gruff raised his eyebrows.

He looked over at the door to make sure no one was about. "I might be able to help you."

Max felt his spirits rise a little. "Really?"

"I've seen some strange things out in the snow," whispered Gruff. "Jim and I were once attacked by this giant ice lizard and you wouldn't find that in any wildlife book. And a cross between a polar bear and a lion once tried to eat me. There are some weird beasts out there. I don't go shouting about them because people would just think I was crazy. But some things can't just be explained away – you know what I mean?"

Max nodded. *What might Gruff know?*

"Anyway," Gruff continued, "when we were filming earlier today, we found an entrance to some sort of ice cave. It didn't look natural – it was like someone had *built* it. And guess what? There were also some weird seven-toed footprints on the ground near the entrance."

Max stood bolt upright. *An ice cave? Might Jenkins be there? And what about* The Triumphant*'s crew?*

"So did you go in?" Max asked.

"We didn't have the right equipment on us," said Gruff, "but we're going back. Why don't you come with us? Maybe that's where Jenkins has been taken. And don't worry about being mauled by these beast things – I can handle anything out there."

Max frowned. "I'll definitely come with you, but I think we should contact emergency services first in case we need back-up."

Gruff shook his head. "If these weird beasts do have her, then getting the emergency services to storm in might make things worse. After all, they've got no experience with things like that. They could put her in even *more* danger."

Max rubbed his eyes, trying to make the right decision. "OK," he nodded, "we check out the cave now. But if Jenkins isn't there, we come straight back and contact the rescue services."

"Definitely," nodded Gruff. "Now let's go!"

A few minutes later, Max found himself down in the storeroom with Gruff and Jim. The blizzard had blown itself out and it was eerily quiet. Jim was stuffing film gear into a large backpack, while Max and Gruff refuelled the three snowmobiles.

As they set out, Max scanned the landscape nervously, expecting some of the snow beasts to appear again. But his determination to rescue Jenkins kept his fear at bay. Plus he had Gruff Addison in his party and Gruff could handle anything. They drove over a mountain and then along the gorge where Gruff and Jim had been filming earlier. After about fifteen minutes, Gruff motioned to Jim and Max with a wave of his arm. They pulled over and got off their snowmobiles.

"It's just up ahead," said Gruff, giving Max an encouraging look. "Don't worry. I bet we'll find her."

They tramped for about twenty metres and then Gruff stopped. "Over here," he said, pointing at an archway cut into the side of a cliff. Max studied it carefully. Gruff was right – it was too neat to have been formed naturally. In the extreme cold, part of the entrance had already iced over.

Max remembered the ice-melting solar panel he'd taken from the research station's roof and reached for his backpack, but Gruff had already pulled out an ice pick. He smashed it against the surface and the ice splintered inwards.

"Come on," he said, replacing the pick in his pack and stepping confidently through the gap.

Max and Jim followed close behind. The three of them found themselves in a short tunnel that led to the top of an icy staircase. Above them were huge, spiked icicles, and sunlight poured through tiny holes in the roof, giving the place an eerie blue glow.

"Wow!" gasped Max in amazement. "What is this place?" He turned to Gruff and Jim, who looked equally awestruck.

"I have no idea," replied Gruff.

"But we're going to find out."

They walked forward and stepped down the staircase. At the bottom were three tunnel openings.

Max took a deep breath. "Which one shall we take?" he asked.

Gruff was about to answer when a deep, bone-chilling howl filled the air. It was coming from the tunnel on the right and was followed by the sound of pounding feet.

Snow beasts!

"SPLIT UP!" commanded Gruff, making for the tunnel on the right. "Jim take the one on the left, Max take the middle one!"

Max was about to question this strategy (was Gruff really going to take on the snow beasts alone?), but Gruff was the survival expert. Jim dived into the left tunnel and Max took the middle one.

The tunnel bent round a corner and then dropped sharply.

MISSION 5

CHAPTER 15

Max crashed downwards, bouncing off the hard icy walls for another hundred metres until he was spat out of the end of the tunnel into a passageway. There was no sign of the other two tunnels, or of Gruff and Jim. Up ahead was a tall archway. He crept forward and stuck his head a fraction round the opening.

He gasped at the sight before him. He was staring into a colossal circular chamber sculpted entirely from ice.

In the centre of the chamber was a huge

console covered in flashing red buttons, dials and silver switches.

Emerging from the top of the console was a wide glass chute, ten metres high. From the mouth of the chute, a gaseous cloud drifted up and out through a large hole in the centre of the chamber's ceiling.

Looking to his right, Max saw that round one semicircle of the chamber's walls were a series of large ice blocks standing in alcoves. From the bottom of each ice block, a red tube spilled out, snaking across the chamber floor and disappearing into a panel on the base of the central console.

Within these blocks he could see dark shapes, but he couldn't make out what they were. Max quickly counted them. There were thirty. Twenty-nine contained shapes; one was empty.

Max looked to his left and saw a selection of industrial thermometers – exactly like the ones at the research station.

So this is where the stolen equipment has got to.

Max gulped as he looked at the displays on the thermometers. They all read −94°C.

This must be where the temperature is being controlled from. But how is it happening exactly?

Max looked up. High above the floor of the chamber was a balcony that circled the entire space. Perched on workstations were computer terminals just like the ones on board *The Triumphant*. There was no sign of any snow beasts, but Max still felt his nerves jangling as he walked round the right side of the chamber. As he reached the ice blocks, he froze and gulped in horror.

Inside each ice block was a human!

At first Max thought all of the people were
dead. But when he looked harder he saw that,
although their bodies were absolutely still,
their eyes were moving from side to side. And
then he saw a face he knew – Captain Edward
Hartnell from *The Triumphant* – he recognized
him from the distress signal Zavonne had
shown him. Max's eyes scanned the row of ice
blocks and saw lots of men wearing naval
uniforms – *The Triumpant*'s crew! The other
trapped people were dressed in explorers' gear.

And in the twenty-ninth block was Dr Stella Jenkins!

Max's brain was in overdrive as he struggled to figure out why these people were being kept prisoner inside ice blocks. *Are the snow beasts carrying out some sort of grotesque experiment?* But his thoughts were suddenly interrupted when he felt a tap on the shoulder. He jumped in terror and spun round, expecting a snow beast attack.

It was Gruff.

Max let out a huge sigh of relief. "You were right," he whispered. "Jenkins is in here and she's not the only prisoner. Let's get these people out and try and get to the bottom of this before the temp hits −100°C."

Gruff didn't move and he didn't say anything.

"COME ON!" Max hissed urgently. "Let's get them out!"

Gruff remained motionless and silent.

"WHAT ARE YOU WAITING FOR?"

Gruff pulled a small vial out of his pocket, containing the green liquid Max had seen Jim drinking earlier. He drank it in one.

And then something weird started to happen. White fur began to spread over Gruff's face. This fur quickly covered his hands, which were transforming into paws with long curved claws. His whole body seemed to increase in size, then his feet burst through his shoes – hairy and seven-toed. His eyes sunk back into their sockets and went a deep shade of crimson with large black pupils.

"*No way!*" uttered Max in horror, as he realized what was happening. He tried to pull away, but Gruff's paw shot out and grabbed him in a vice-like grip.

MISSION 5

CHAPTER 17

"GET OFF ME!" yelled Max, struggling like mad as he stared in horror at the 'new' Gruff.

"We've been keeping an eye on you from the second you visited *The Triumphant*," snarled Gruff in a deep, guttural voice, his hot, salty breath on Max's face. He pushed his face into Max's, his crimson eyes flashing with anger.

"So it was you who made those ice holes that nearly killed me!" said Max.

"Those under-ice explosives we took from *The Triumphant* have their uses," growled

Gruff, "but they obviously weren't enough to throw you off our trail."

"And the avalanche..." muttered Max.

"Again, you were lucky," hissed Gruff.

"What are you doing with all of these people?" demanded Max, as Gruff's luminous eyes bore into him.

Gruff shoved Max forward until they were just a few metres away from the ice blocks. As they got nearer, Max got a much clearer view of the trapped humans. Their faces were so pale they were almost transparent.

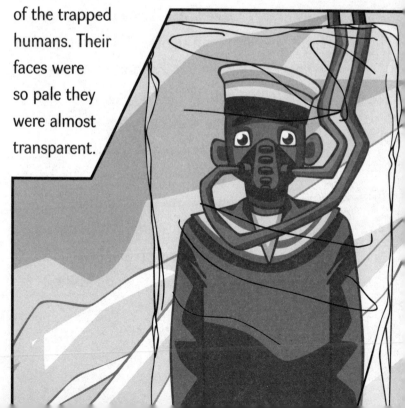

Each prisoner wore some kind of mask, with a red and a blue tube running from it. Max noticed that the blue tube entered each ice block through its roof. Gruff followed his gaze and laughed – a harsh, grating cackle.

"Oh yes, we *do* feed them. Those blue tubes provide just enough nutrients to keep them alive, and their bodies are kept at just the right temperature not to kill them."

"Why are you keeping humans alive in blocks of ice?" yelled Max, struggling again.

Gruff squeezed him tightly. "Well, as our plan is so near to completion, I suppose there's no harm in telling you. We need their CO_2."

Max stared at the red tubes coming out of the base of the ice blocks and leading to the central console.

"To achieve our goal we need to collect CO_2 from humans," went on Gruff. "We combine the gas they breathe out with a special concoction of chemical compounds in the console and when mixed together they produce *that*!"

Gruff pointed at the cloud of gas rising up from the console and out through the hole in the chamber's roof.

"I get it," said Max bitterly. "It's the gas that's lowering the temperature."

"Got it in one!" roared Gruff. "For our plan to be finalized, we need the temperature to fall to –100°C, but unfortunately we have a little problem. And that's where you come in."

Max looked at the thermometers stuck at –94°C. "Your console's broken down and you want me to fix it?" asked Max hopefully.

"The console is fine!" shouted Gruff, revealing sharp yellow teeth. "And now it is time for the spectacle to begin."

Gruff clapped his hands and high up in the chamber at least a hundred snow beasts began to appear, each taking a place on the balcony, with a perfect view of the chamber floor.

"W-w-what are you doing?" asked Max nervously, as a hundred pairs of hate-filled crimson eyes gazed down at him.

"MY FRIENDS!" roared Gruff, gazing up at the balcony. "THE TIME HAS FINALLY COME TO COMPLETE OUR PROJECT!"

There was an outbreak of cheering and whooping.

Gruff turned back to face Max. "The problem is that we haven't been able to collect quite enough CO_2."

I don't like where this is going.

"But we now have the last human we need to finish the job," said Gruff, grinning hideously at Max. "YOU!"

CHAPTER 18

Max gulped nervously. Gruff was now in full swing.

"You humans thought we were just a myth – yetis, Bigfoot and the rest of us. But we're as real as you!"

Gruff spat out the words.

"During the Ice Age *we* were the ones who inhabited the earth's surface. There was glorious snow and ice everywhere. It was delightfully freezing and we had thousands of miles in which we could roam. But as the earth warmed up, we were forced to retreat underground to small, icy chasms. Yes, it was cold enough down there for us to stay alive, but we were cramped and uncomfortable! You humans with your planet warming have kept us down there for thousands and thousands of years. Well, now it is time for the big freeze. When the temperature reaches −100°C the change will be irreversible and it will be cold enough for us to return to the surface." Gruff looked up at the balcony. "Welcome to the NEW ICE AGE!"

There were thunderous claps and screams from the snow beasts. Max's mind whirred furiously.

Gruff hadn't been fixing the heating system back at the research station – he was making sure it stayed broken to keep the indoor temperature as cold as possible for himself! And that's why he must have been at the station. He was in a perfect place to steal

equipment. Plus the snow beasts stole loads of equipment from The Triumphant – *not to mention the entire crew!*

"This new Ice Age will make the earth a home for us," shouted Gruff. "And for the yetis and Bigfoot and even Alfred – the one you humans call the Abominable Snow Man."

Alfred?!

Max suddenly heard a loud clanking noise behind him. He twisted round and saw two snow beasts pushing a trolley that held an ice block like the others, although this one was in two hollowed-out halves.

Max shuddered.

"Isn't it wonderful?" roared Gruff, playing to the gallery. "This stupid human boy thought he could stop us, but he'll end up being the one who gives us the extra CO_2 we need to complete the job! Why else does he think we led him here – for an iced tea party?"

There were screams of high-pitched laughter

from the balcony. Gruff clapped his paws and the laughter stopped immediately.

He lunged towards Max and lifted him clean off the ground. Max struggled and wriggled like crazy, but Gruff's grip was unbelievably strong.

"Say hello to your new home!" said Gruff, with a hideous grin. "We trust you'll be comfortable in there!"

"LET GO OF ME!" screamed Max, as Gruff dropped him into one half of the ice block. Before Max could make a move, one of the snow beasts fastened a mask to his face. Gruff then heaved the other half of the block and dropped it on to the first. As the halves connected, Max heard a loud click and the two parts of the ice block became one. The thirtieth prisoner was now firmly in place.

MISSION 5

CHAPTER 19

"NOOOOO!" yelled Max from inside his prison. The ice was so densely packed around him that he could hardly move. He cursed under his breath – breath that was sending his CO_2 out through the tube and straight into the central console. Max watched in horror as the thermometers around the chamber suddenly dropped from -94°C to -95°C.

Max's body shook with rage (in an extremely cramped fashion). *Gruff's right – it will be my CO_2 that's going to finish the job for them!*

He cursed himself for ever trusting Gruff. Mind you, Gruff's cover as a TV survival expert had been absolutely brilliant – it hadn't just convinced Max, it had fooled millions of people the world over.

OK, I'm not going to stop them from inside this ice block so I have to get out. But how?

Max moved his lips a couple of centimetres forward and took a sip from the blue tube. He sucked in a sugary liquid that tasted a bit like a flat fizzy drink.

Bearable but not my future choice of beverage!

Max forced himself to relax his body as much as possible and tried to lower his right arm. It moved a few millimetres but no more; he was freeze-packed like a Christmas turkey! He tried his left arm and, to his relief, there was a tiny bit more room for manoeuvre on this side. He pressed his left arm against his body with all his might, then stretched it down as far as he could. It was agonizingly slow, but his fingers finally reached his snowsuit pocket.

He looked out at the chamber. The thermometers had just reached −96°C.

I need to do this fast!

Max inched his hand inside the pocket and curled his fingers around the ICE-CUTTER HEADPHONES. As he did this he remembered Zavonne's information.

If this ice is any thicker than 50 centimetres, the cutters won't work.

Out in the chamber, Gruff was flicking switches and issuing muffled instructions to the beasts up in the balcony.

Taking a deep breath, Max pushed his whole body back as hard as he could. This provided just about enough space in front of him for the next stage of his plan.

Max lifted the headphones up in front of him and held them approximately thirty centimetres apart. He looked out of the ice block, and his heart sank when he saw the thermometers move again, to −97°C.

He pushed the headphones against the ice block's surface. For a few seconds nothing happened, but just as despair was about to engulf Max he heard a faint crackling sound and saw a large circle appear in the ice. He could see that if he pushed the circle, it would topple forward and leave a big enough gap for him to squeeze through.

But Gruff was on the chamber floor and there were a hundred other beasts dotted round the balcony. As soon as Max escaped, they would be on to him in seconds.

As he frantically tried to think of a way to distract Gruff and the snow beasts, the thermometers made a sickening movement; −98°C.

Max gulped.

Time was almost up.

MISSION 5

CHAPTER 20

*Never in the history of the world has anyone
needed a decoy as badly as I do at this
precise second.*

In a state of desperation, Max suddenly had
a brainwave. He pushed his lips towards the
dangling blue tube and, instead of sucking,
blew into it as hard as he could. A large red
light on a steel wall panel on the other side of
the chamber began to flash and a harsh alarm
blared out. Max saw Gruff run over to the
panel and he seized his chance.

Squashing his fists together, he pushed the circle he'd made in the wall of the ice block. There was a creaking sound and it fell forward, thudding on to the chamber floor. Max twisted his body, pushed himself out of the ice block and tore off his mask. All eyes were fixed on the flashing panel and he had almost reached the central console by the time the snow beasts spotted him.

"THE BOY HAS ESCAPED!" hollered the beasts from the balcony.

Max ran on towards the console, his heart pulsating wildly.

Gruff threw himself across the chamber towards Max and reached out to seize his ankles. But Max swerved out of the way and launched himself through the air. He grabbed hold of a steel lever on the surface of the console and used this to begin his ascent up the side.

"ATTACK HIM!" screeched Gruff, and a split

second
later, Max
felt a sharp
pain in his back.
He looked up to see
the beasts on the
balcony pulling icicles
from the chamber walls and
hurling them at him. One of
these icy spears hit him on the
shoulder and he cried out in pain. But
he grabbed on to another lever on the
console and pulled himself up further
towards the base of the glass chute.

As more icicles flew down towards him,
Max lashed out with his feet to kick as many
off course as possible. But still one hit his
right arm and another smashed against the
back of his legs, almost causing him to lose
his footing. He reached the base of the chute

As icicles rained down on him, Max reached into his backpack and pulled out the small solar panel. He threw it high into the air. His aim was spot on – the panel flew into the mouth of the chute. He heard it crashing down against the sides of the chute and then come to a stop.

Immediately the shaft of sunlight shining down through the hole in the chamber's roof made contact with the solar panel. But when Max spun round to check the thermometers he groaned: –99°C. He'd done his best, but was it too late?

MISSION 5

CHAPTER 21

As Max stared up at the chute deciding his next move, there was suddenly a gasp of shock from every snow beast in the chamber. Max glanced at the thermometers again. They had stopped at −99°C. Max held his breath. Ten seconds later, the reading changed.

But this time *in the other direction*.

The thermometers returned to −98°C. Max's eyes widened.

"DESTROY HIM!" shrieked Gruff. A fresh wave of icicles smashed against Max, but he ignored the pain because the thermometers changed again. They went up to –97°C and then in quick succession to –96°C and –95°C.

Yesssssssssss! The solar panel is doing the trick! It's warming up the freezing concoction inside the console!

Max looked down and saw that Gruff was standing by the console, frantically trying to open a hatch on its side to retrieve the solar panel. But however hard Gruff pulled it wouldn't budge, and the temperature continued to rise.

And then Max felt a couple of drips on his forehead. He looked up and saw that the chamber's icy roof was beginning to melt. Still the temperature rose. The drips started falling faster and it wasn't long before they'd turned into drops. Max leaped down from the console and landed on the chamber floor.

Console dealt with. Now it's time to free the prisoners.

As the temperature hit −55°C, Max heard groans coming from the beasts on the balconies.

The temperature is getting too warm for them!

A couple of chunks of the chamber wall became dislodged and fell down. Max sidestepped them and ran across to the ice blocks. He'd almost reached them when he heard the beasts' groans become tortured howls. He looked back and saw several beasts leaping down from the balcony, then lying on the chamber floor in an attempt to keep themselves as cold as possible.

Max skidded to avoid a falling beast and ran to Jenkins's ice-block prison. He pushed at its top half a couple of times but it didn't budge, so he shoulderbarged the block and smashed the top clean off.

He helped a freezing and terrified Jenkins to climb out.

"You need to get the others out of here as fast as possible," he instructed Jenkins.

"B-b-but y-y-you a-a-are..." she stuttered, still shivering.

"Forget about me," commanded Max. "There's a small opening in the chamber wall over there, where the ice is melting."

And even though Jenkins could only shuffle slowly, she made it to the next ice block and helped Captain Hartnell kick open a hole through the slushy surface. Then together they started freeing the others.

As Max turned back to face the centre of the chamber, he saw that a huge opening had appeared in the floor. Snow beasts were rapidly flinging themselves into it.

That must lead back down to the icy chasms Gruff spoke about!

The thermometers now read −40°C, and Max felt a streak of satisfaction. But this was short-lived, as he suddenly felt a powerful hand wrap itself around his throat.

"NOW YOU'LL SEE WHAT A REAL PRISON FEELS LIKE!" screamed Gruff.

MISSION 5

CHAPTER 22

Gruff gripped Max firmly and dragged him towards the opening. Huge chunks of ice were now smashing down on to the chamber floor and the rest of the beasts were diving into the ice chasms. And as the hole widened further the central console dropped out of sight, too.

"You may have wrecked our plan," barked Gruff, "but you're going down with us!"

Max shuddered as he imagined what it would be like in the freezing chasms deep

below the earth. Realizing he had but a few
seconds to save himself, he suddenly reached
out, grabbed a handful of fur on Gruff's chest
and pulled it as hard as he could.

"Aaaarrrgggghhhhhh!" screeched Gruff,
letting go of Max and twisting in pain. Max
leaned forward and shoved Gruff on the back.
Gruff toppled over and with a cry of,
"YOU HAVEN'T HEARD THE LAST
OF THIS!" tumbled
into the hole.

Torrents of water were now gushing down, as Max ran towards the hole through which Jenkins and Captain Hartnell had led the other prisoners. But Max's path was suddenly blocked. Towering over him was a snow beast whose dark crimson eyes scorched with venom. Max spotted something in his hand – a video camera. It was Jim!

"Gruff may have failed, but I won't!" he roared, puffing out his chest and reaching for Max. Max ducked and Jim swiped the air, dropping his camera to the ground.

Without wasting a second, Max grabbed the camera and whacked it against Jim's back. It flew out of his hands and skidded after Jim, across the chamber floor and down into the huge hole. Max dived out of the way as a massive chunk of ice crashed to the ground.

Time for a quick exit!

But the way out was now blocked by the chunk of ice.

Max sprinted towards the wall of ice and kicked out as hard as he could. He knocked out a small opening and dived through. He hit the ground outside, picked himself up and started running. A split second later the entire ceiling collapsed, along with the chamber walls.

Max turned round and stared at the giant mound of snow and melting ice. If he hadn't been inside the chamber, he wouldn't have believed it had ever existed. He turned round and up ahead saw a group of freezing and exhausted people. He ran over to them and located Jenkins.

"W-w-who ... are you?" she mouthed through chattering lips.

Mindful of the need to keep his identity secret, Max replied, "No one," before leaping on to one of the snowmobiles and speeding back to the research station. As soon as he was inside, he grabbed the satellite communications equipment and contacted the emergency services. His call was picked up instantly and he issued his instructions. "We need as many helicopters and personnel as you can spare to the following co-ordinates in the Bolt Zone..."

MAX FLASH

MISSION 5

CHAPTER 23

Three hours later, Max went to say goodbye to Dr Klosh and Dr Holroyd.

"Bye guys, thanks for all your help," said Max.

The scientists nodded. "The temperature now seems to have stabilized," said Klosh, turning to Holroyd.

Oh well, what did I expect?

Max made his way out to where the DFEA helicopter was waiting, hovering above the ground. He climbed up the ladder. The pilot gave him a thumbs-up and they sped off.

At the airport, while Max was waiting for his plane flight home, a news bulletin on a screen in the departure lounge caught his attention.

"News has come in of a major search and rescue operation in an area of the Antarctic known as the Bolt Zone," announced the newsreader.

Max's eyes lit up.

"We're hearing that among those rescued were the captain and crew of the stricken British navy vessel *The Triumphant*—"

The newsreader pulled an incredulous face.

"I've just been handed an update stating that a number of explorers who vanished without trace in the region – some as far back as two *years* ago – were also among the survivors. They were exceptionally cold, but remarkably none of them were suffering from hypothermia. The survivors have been relaying all kinds of stories – talking about being frozen in ice blocks by strange Yeti-like creatures. One of them, a Dr

Stella Jenkins, spoke of how a remarkable boy managed to free everyone. On the line we have Dr Tarquin Carruthers – a psychology specialist in extreme-weather survivors. Dr Carruthers, what do you make of these statements?"

"People who suffer long periods of incarceration in the snow often speak in a nonsensical fashion when they're freed. I call this post-ice-babble."

"What about these reports of a mystery boy?"

"This 'boy' is no more than a figment of their imaginations – he's a symbol of their freedom. It will be interesting to hear what the survivors have to say once their bodies and minds have returned to their usual temperatures."

The newsreader moved on to another report and Max turned away from the screen.

Hmm, I managed to free everyone and stop the temperature reaching −100°C, but have I blown my cover?

MAX FLASH
MISSION 5
CHAPTER 24

On touch-down, a taxi was waiting for Max and it wasn't long before he was home. His mum gave him an almighty hug when he came in through the front door.

"We saw the reports on the news," she said. "We're incredibly proud of you."

"M-u-m," said Max, extricating himself from her grasp.

"She's right," beamed his dad, squeezing Max's shoulder affectionately. "It sounds like you did a first-class job out there."

"I did my best," replied Max.

"Zavonne wants you down in the Communications Centre for an immediate debrief," said Mum.

Max was in no hurry to see Zavonne, and by the time he made his way down there, her face was already on the large plasma screen.

I just hope I'm not in too much trouble!

"I'm not very happy about you damaging one of the snowmobiles," was Zavonne's opening comment.

I don't like where this is going...

"Luckily for you, though, Dr Jenkins has been told you left the region well before her 'escape' and she is now fully convinced she was hallucinating down in the ice chamber. She's also sure that her capture by the snow beasts was also invented by her traumatized mind."

Thank goodness for that.

"I take it that Doctors Holroyd and Klosh don't suspect your involvement in any of this?"

"They're too wrapped up in their research," replied Max.

"Am I right in understanding that the snow beasts' infrastructure was totally destroyed and that all of them returned to their ice chasms? And that the temperature in the Bolt Zone has returned to normal?"

Max nodded.

"Well, that's something," noted Zavonne through pursed lips.

A thought struck Max. "Er, Zavonne?"

"Yes?"

"You know my Californian holiday was cut short, and I missed out on all of that sun and surfing? Well, does the DFEA have any sort of compensation package? You know – something to make up for my lost watersports time?"

Zavonne thought about this for a few seconds.

At last, I'm going to get something decent out of her!

A metal drawer on the wall started flashing.
"Look inside," instructed Zavonne.

Max pulled the drawer open expectantly and
picked out a small rectangle of card with
writing on one side:

> This ticket entitles the owner to one free forty-five
> minute session at their local swimming baths.

As Zavonne's face vanished from the screen,
Max groaned.

Unbelievable!

As he tramped up the stairs, half of him was
furious with Zavonne for her ingratitude. But
the other half was already waiting for her next
summons. For Max Flash the next mission
couldn't come soon enough.

EPILOGUE

Miles beneath the earth's surface a large crowd of snow beasts sat squashed together in a freezing, cramped and dimly-lit ice chasm.

"Look on the bright side," said Jim, "we *nearly* made it. If that kid had been a minute later with the solar panel stunt, we'd have been sipping snow cocktails from ice glasses now."

"*Nearly* isn't good enough!" snapped Gruff. "I should've stayed with my TV job – it beats being stuck down here."

"Hang on a second," said Jim. "My camera fell down with me. We can still make films. What do you say?"

"Films about what?" griped Gruff. "The darkness and boredom we're going to experience over the next million years."

"That's a starting point," grinned Jim, grabbing his camera.

Gruff sighed wearily. "OK, I'll do it."

"Just smooth down your fur on top a bit," instructed Jim.

Gruff patted his fur. "Better?" he asked.

Jim gave him a thumbs-up and pressed the standby button.

Gruff cleared his throat and pulled his most winning TV smile.

"And action!" called Jim.

FUTURISTIC ROBOTS ARE IN TOWN WITH DEADLY INTENTIONS!